LULU
and the
FLYING BABIES

also by Posy Simmonds

FRED

FOR:

Tim, Mike, Annie, Clare,
Lucy, Douglas, Juliet,
James, Anna, and Rupert

This is a Borzoi Book published by Alfred A. Knopf, Inc.

Copyright © 1988 by Posy Simmonds.
All rights reserved under International and Pan-American Copyright Conventions. Published in the United
States by Alfred A. Knopf, Inc., New York. Distributed by Random House, Inc., New York.
Published in Great Britain by Jonathan Cape Limited, London.
First American Edition. Manufactured in Italy.
1 3 5 7 9 10 8 6 4 2

Library of Congress Cataloging-in-Publication Data
Simmonds, Posy.
Lulu and the flying babies / by Posy Simmonds. p. cm.
Summary: Stuck waiting for her family in the art museum when she would much rather be playing outside
in the park, a little girl is picked up by two cherubim and taken for a wild romp through several paintings.
ISBN 0-394-89597-5   ISBN 0-394-99597-X (lib. bdg.)
[1. Angels—Fiction.   2. Art museums—Fiction.   3. Museums—Fiction.   4. Cartoons and comics.]
I. Title. PZ7.S5913Lu 1988 [E]—dc19 87-15889

POSY SIMMONDS

LULU

and the
FLYING BABIES

ALFRED A. KNOPF ✧ NEW YORK

I was angry at home....

I was angry in the street....

WHEN are we....going to the **PA-ARK**?!

I was angry in the park...

I shouted in the museum....

And when you feel better...

...you come and find us by the dinosaur over there...see...

Don't pick your nose!

And use your hanky....not your sleeve!

Don't sniff!

And don't stand on the SEAT!

We rolled in the snow.....

We splashed in the sea....

We growled at a tiger.....

We patted a King....and gave crisps to his horse.....

We ate some cherries......

...and apples and plums...

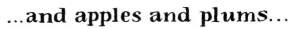

...and we spat out the stones down a mountain side....

We got lost in a dark, scary wood.

INFORMATION

Lost, eh?

Tell me, what do your mummy and daddy look like?

Well...*HIS* mummy's wearing a pink nightie and she's riding a **COW**.....

Riding a COW!?

...and his daddy's got a big **FORK** and **grapes** on his head.....

Eh?

Good gracious me! ......and **YOUR** Daddy?...What about **HIM**?

...My daddy.... he's got a woolly hat...and he's carrying my baby brother.....

And here he is!

Lulu!

Deh!

I hugged my Dad and kissed my baby brother...

And *where* did you get to?

Now.. what about you...**TWO**!?

Oh, I *know* **YOU**!

HOW did you get out?

Now, you come along with me...

I went with *flying babies!*

FLYING BABIES?!

I DID!

Hey! Where've they gone?

There **WERE** flying babies! They've gone!

Fancy that!

We splashed in the sea..we growled at a tiger...we...

We rolled in the snow!

I flew with them! I **did!**

...**we patted** a **king!** We spat plum stones down a mountain...we got lost in a dark, scary wood....we....

Well I never!